The diary of
A 1960s TEENAGER

To Christine, Eve, Gerry and Janet,
who lent me their memories.

Editor Louisa Sladen
Editor-in-Chief John C. Miles
Designer Jason Billin/Billin Design Solutions
Art Director Jonathan Hair

First published in 2001
by Franklin Watts
96 Leonard Street
London
EC2A 4XD

Franklin Watts Australia
56 O'Riordan Street
Alexandria
NSW 2015

ISBN 0 7496 4258 0 (hbk)
0 7496 4420 6 (pbk)

Dewey classification: 941.085

A CIP catalogue record for this book is available
from the British Library.

Printed in Great Britain

The diary of A 1960s TEENAGER

by Moira Butterfield
Illustrated by Brian Duggan

All about this book

This is the fictional diary of an eighteen-year-old girl called Jane Leachman. She starts her story in 1965 when she moves from Coventry to London to start a career in fashion.

What's so special about the 1960s?

The 1960s was a decade of great change in Britain. People began to think differently about many things, from how society should work to what was right and wrong in everyday behaviour.

Pop music, fashion and television became more popular than ever before, along with all kinds of new home gadgets that made life easier. By the end of the decade people dressed, lived and thought very differently to people in the 1950s.

Change happened fast and every year in the 1960s was unique. This diary covers 1965 and 1966, when the Beatles were a smash hit, the miniskirt appeared and London was hailed around the world as the "swinging" capital of style. During 1967 hippy styles in music and fashion arrived, but that was after the time period covered by this diary.

Do you know any Sixties guys or chicks?

The best way to find out about the 1960s is to ask people who lived through it. To help with this book the author gathered true stories from people who were teenagers in the years from 1965 to 1966. For instance, somebody *did* say: "With a stupid name like that, the Beatles will never be a success!"

Become a hip historian yourself by asking adults you know if they can remember the 1960s. They might be able to tell you their own unique memories about their home, family and friends.

Money in 1965

You'll see that Jane writes amounts of money differently in her diary to the way we do today. That's because in the 1960s Britain had pre-decimal coinage, not the money that we use today. A pound was made up of twenty shillings. Each shilling was made up of twelve pence.

Pennies were written with a "d" (short for the Latin word *denarius*), not with a "p" as they are today. Something that cost six pence would have been written 6d.

This diary belongs to
Jane Leachman

History according
to
me

18 AUGUST 1965

Things are changing fast around here. History in the making, as they say. Buildings going up, prices going up and skirts definitely going way up. Mum's given me this diary in the hope that I'll catch some of this history and trap it before it disappears. The way things are moving I'll have to be quick.

So here goes, with what I consider the most important event of 1965 so far... I've just finished writing a job application. It makes me sound so very grown-up, doesn't it? Well, I suppose I am eighteen and I did leave school three years ago, but I've never felt like an adult. Not like a real rent-paying, bill-paying adult. Not like Mum and Dad. I suppose that's why I'm doing something nutty like going for a job that will change my life out of all recognition. Change. It's a big thing.

"Hold on, Jane. You haven't got the job yet," as Dad would no doubt say, but I want it more than anything I've ever wanted. I must do because it'll mean I have to move away from home, but it'll be worth it. Everyone is saying that London is the most exciting town on the whole of the planet. In the galaxy! Compared to Coventry it's in another universe.

Of course it's unheard of round here for girls to leave home before they get married, let alone swan off to new universes. I'm going to do things differently.

This morning Mr Binton from next door stuck his head over the fence to complain about my brother Dave and his friends making a noise with their scooters. I tell him I've applied for a job and he starts muttering about "Women working…taking jobs away from those that need 'em." Mrs Binton smiles sweetly and adds: "I suppose it'll keep you occupied until you're married and children come along. Don't leave it too long, duckie." She refers to all unmarried women over twenty as "on the shelf", making them sound like dusty old teapots. She's way, way out of date. Hasn't she heard that things are changing?

21 August 1965

Interview day. I borrow Mum's best "Paris Look" outfit, a sensible skirt and jacket that makes me look like the wife of an American president. I decide to jazz it up with my black and white plastic mac, Hush Puppies and white lipstick.

"Are you sure you should wear that lipstick

to an interview, Jane?" asks Dad.

"Of course, Dad. Get with it!" I try to sound confident, but will it be the with-it look at Kilter and Kilter, traditional tailors, 120 West End Lane, London NW6? ("Bespoke clothing with quality service.")

Will they require a new general assistant who spends her waking hours studying every fashion magazine going and wants more than anything to make minidresses with the bit over the tummy cut out?

We leave home unbelievably early and chug towards London in Dad's car, his pride and joy and the only one in our street. He likes to be modern, our dad.

"Mark my words, Jane. Everyone will have a car one day, a British one made in Coventry."

The journey seems to take so long we could have started from Australia. Around about Watford, I start feeling very nervous and I wipe off the white lipstick.

24 August 1965

A letter arrives from Kilter and Kilter, in my opinion, the two most wonderful old gents that ever waved a pair of dressmaking scissors. They are offering "remuneration" of £4 a week.

I look up "remuneration" in the dictionary and realise it means that I'll be rich, but only for a few minutes, before I have to pay for rent and food and end up stony broke again. I've been offered a flatshare above the tailor's shop, with a girl called Kay Parkinson. With a name like that she must be posh.

Mum and Dad are brilliant about it all.

"It'll be good for you to stand on your own two feet. You know where we are if you need us."

Dave is pleased because he thinks that now Dad will have to agree to him being in a pop band.

"I never had any money like that when I was your age," says Mum. "Don't go mad with it. You should save. A shilling doesn't go far these days." And she's off on a lecture about the price of eggs, a shocking shilling a dozen apparently.

I've noticed all parents say the same things:

"Kids have it easy these days. They don't know they're born."

"Have you seen the state of those pop stars? You can't tell whether they're boys or girls."

"They'll never make it with a stupid name like 'the Beatles'."

"You make sure you get home by ten thirty, young lady, or you'll end up a bad lot."

"That's not music. It's just shouting."

All of us teenagers say:

"Mum! Dad! You're embarrassing me!"

28 AUGUST 1965

Dave turns seventeen and we go to the Palais Dance Hall to celebrate. All the boys are dressed like Beatles and the girls have tried as best they can to look like the sort of chicks that might hang out with Paul McCartney. All in all, we don't look half bad.

29 AUGUST 1965

When Mrs Binton hears that I'm going to live away in London she is open-mouthed for a while, and then says: "Oh dearie me," as if I've caught a disease. Mr Binton is particularly horrible.

"You be careful where you end up, young lady. There are coloureds moving in everywhere, comin' in from the Commonwealth. Shouldn't be allowed. I wouldn't let a girl of mine near 'em."

"Coloured people are OK. They're just like you and me, I hope I meet lots of them," I reply angrily.

"Well, of all the nerve! Teenagers these days! You should have more respect for your elders, young lady," he spits out pompously. I hope that one day the miserable old git chokes on a mouldy pork pie.

3 September 1965

Official diary announcement:
Jane Leachman is now a Londoner, along with Cockneys, the Queen and a million pigeons. She is to be found pattern-cutting, cutting material and making up outfits in the workshop of Kilter and Kilter.

So what does it look like, this new universe? Out front there's a shop that leads on to a busy street. It's kept tidy by Mr Benjamin Kilter. At the back the workshop is crowded with rolls of cloth, boxes of cotton reels, sewing machines, tailors' dummies, dressmaking tape and all sorts of other things with or without names. There's hardly room for me plus Mr Henry Kilter (brother of Mr Kilter B.) and nephew Percy, who's a couple of years older than I am. Mr Kilter H. has a catchphrase like a man on one of the telly quizzes: "There's lots to learn. Lots to learn."

But Percy can't wait. He confides in me that he's itching to update the family business.

"I want Kilter and Kilter to be modern, right there in the spotlight, on the magazine covers. What my uncles don't get is that fashion's changing week by week. We should be in the groove."

Percy is one of those small but energy-filled people. He has unruly floppy hair that he pushes back with his fingers as he thinks at a hundred miles an hour. He usually wears Beatle boots, trousers and a polo neck in some sort of nylon ("Man-made fabrics are where it's at, Jane.") Oh, and he wants to change his name: "Because everyone does these days." When a customer came in to the shop this morning he introduced himself as "Justin", and would have carried it off if Mr Kilter H. hadn't called out from the back: "Percy, can you sort out a gusset, pronto?"

I like Percy because he feels as passionately about fashion as I do, and so I tell him my ambition to be a top designer. It turns out we have the same dream of success.

"We could be a team!" he cries. "Lots of designers work in teams. I can see our names in lights, can't you?" And I have to say that yes, I think I can.

I'm installed in the flat above the workshop with my new flatmate, Kay Parkinson, a distant cousin of Percy's. We're sharing the rent of £3 10/- a week. At first I thought we looked so opposite, we couldn't possibly get on. Kay's got a fabulous figure, elegant and willowy. She looks sensational in anything she wears and seems as effortlessly stylish as any society hostess. I'm tall and thick-set, more like an oak than a willow! Kay is just starting a career as a model, and she's got fabulous blonde hair that swings when she walks, not like my poker-straight ginger lion's mane. But you shouldn't judge by appearances, and Kay turns out to be kind and full of fun, not toffee-nosed at all.

"Don't hide your freckles, Jane. They're cute. Jane Asher has them and she goes out with Paul McCartney."

See why I like her? Percy, Kay and me are soon good friends and take to calling ourselves "The Groovy Gang". We don't have boyfriends or girlfriends, money or fame (yet) but we do share the ambition to make it in this big old town. All for one and one for all. The three musketeers – Sixties style!

10 September 1965

I have my own news correspondent, a cheerful chap called Norman. He sells newspapers from a booth near Kilters' and now he knows me he gives me a wave whenever I go by. All I have to say is "What's new, Norman?" and he gives me a personal news update:

"America's in hot water on page one. They've had street riots over the colour of people's skin.

It seems that some white people won't mix with black people, on buses, in schools or on beaches even. Black people are trying to change things, and there's been big trouble over it."

"On page two Prime Minister Harold Wilson is predicting that Labour will get back in come the next election, so he'll be able to stay in Downing Street a bit longer. On page seven they say plastic hats are all the rage, and on the back page they say Bobby Charlton is the world's best footballer. I won't argue with that. Have a good day, darlin'. Make me a new pair of trousers, eh?"

13 September 1965

Kay and I have jazzed up our flat, kitting it out with plastic chairs and a rug. There's a telly in a wooden cabinet like the one at home, but we've updated it by covering the top with orange sticky-back plastic. We finished the look by making some giant tissue-paper flowers, but now we're spoiling the whole effect by draping our wet washing everywhere. We end the day munching chips and watching a TV quiz show with an amazing prize of a thousand pounds. With money like that you could buy a whole house in Coventry, but I'm not sure I'd want to now. I miss Mum and Dad, of course, but every day I wake up excited to think I've got my own place. I wouldn't mind a thousand pounds, though...

16 September 1965

Kay tells me there's another tailor in the street called Freddie Fortune, who's taken to calling himself a "gear designer".

When I ask Mr Kilter H. about him, the old gent chuckles. "Freddie Fortune! Is that what he's calling himself now? I think you'll find he was christened Bert Crump. He's got a lot to learn, a lot to learn, that boy."

17 September 1965

I'm walking along with Percy at lunchtime when a man in dangerously tight trousers walks out of the fish and chip shop. He is long and gangly, and reminds me of a daddy-long-legs. His unnaturally black hair looks stiff with hairspray.

"Percy!" he shouts, over loudly, so everyone can hear. "How are your gussets? Still working in tweed?" He giggles and I decide I definitely don't like him.

"Hello, dearie," he turns to me. "Helping out the old tailors are you? You should take a look at my place – "Freddie Fortune's Gear Emporium". I design clothes. I don't just cobble them together from old pattern pieces." He swaggers off, leaving Percy purple with rage and frustration.

"He can't...he can't..." Percy is lost for words.

"He can't even sew a seam properly," says Mr Kilter H. when I tell him what happened in the street. "We had him helping in here once, but he walked out. Too grand to sweep up."

Percy overhears.

"Yes, but at least he does up-to-date clothes – gear!" He seems near to tears.

5 OCTOBER 1965

The big news is we're working hard to get some clothes samples ready for a presentation to Plimptons, West End department store, no less. ("Purveyors of fine goods since 1860.") Their buyer, Mrs Diggins, sometimes chooses Kilter-made items to stock.

Plimptons are rather old-fashioned, and we're making up traditional jacket, trousers and skirt samples for Mrs Diggins to choose from. "These styles are just like what people wore during the war," Percy moans, and I secretly agree. Couldn't they sell a miniskirt or two? I can't pluck up the courage to ask the uncles, though, in case I lose my job.

Kay decides to cheer me up by taking me shopping. We look longingly through the window of Bazaar Boutique on the King's Road (too expensive for us). Kay thinks she sees the famous owner, Mary Quant, standing in a coffee bar wearing a miniskirt. She designs the hottest clothes around, but Biba, the boutique in Kensington, is more our scene because it's cheaper but still very with-it. I find a pair of multicoloured tights, and a bright yellow minidress with metal links holding the top and bottom together. It has to be the trendiest outfit I've ever owned.

"You'll catch your death," I can hear my mum saying, but I don't care. I have to have it!

15 October 1965

PARTY!

We're all going to a party in a flat up the road. Kay got invited by a bloke she met in the greengrocers. No man can resist her, even when she's buying cabbages. He got more than he bargained for because she said she would only accept if she could bring her groovy gang – i.e: me and Percy. All for one and one for all! Apparently this bloke's got no chance anyway, since Kay says she doesn't have time for boyfriends.

"Maybe in a few years I might settle down, when I'm rich and famous. But right now I'm too busy having fun! Don't you agree?"

I agree. Besides, looking like a groovy chick takes up all my time, what with false eyelashes to stick on and white plastic boots to clean. I've gotta look good for my first swinging London party.

16 October 1965

THE PARTY REPORT

by Jane Leachman, reporter on the spot.

Scores out of 10 :

* Clothes of guests: 9 (one man wore a tweed jacket and gentlemen's club tie)

* Food: 8 (I liked the cheese cubes on sticks but not the stale Twiglets)

* Drinks: 7 (Beer and Wine.) I thought wine was very sophisticated until I tasted it. It was just like Gran's pickling vinegar.

* Venue: 6 - Crowded small house with everyone crammed in corridors, kitchen and on the stairs. An outside toilet, only to be attempted using the house torch.
* Music: 10 - The Beatles, The Dave Clark Five, The Kinks etc. The Rolling Stones sound cool.
* Guests: 10 - All sorts! (see below)

My evening:

We arrive, pushing our way in through the crowded hallway. I feel a little nervous, expecting everyone to be very cool and with-it. I straighten my minidress, munch a pickled onion (possibly a mistake) and start by talking to:

Adam:

He loves politics and rabbits on about it non-stop. He thinks that just because things are old and traditional it doesn't mean we shouldn't question them – the monarchy, for instance. He obviously hasn't asked my gran, who would have no hesitation in chasing him over the White Cliffs of Dover with her royal souvenir umbrella.

According to Adam, young Americans are much cooler than we are because they've been out on the streets demonstrating about their troops going to fight in Vietnam, and they really want to change things. When he starts on about "oppression of the proletariat" I realise he hasn't let me get a word in edgeways, so I decide to change things myself by getting away from him, only to bump into:

Baz:

He turns out to be a bit too modern, even for me, when he suggests that because it's an all-night party we could get more friendly in the back room on top of the coat pile. Then he tries to kiss me and I feel pleased that I ate that pickled onion. I say "No thanks," as politely but firmly as I can.

"Come on, this is the Sixties, love. Let it all hang out. Anything goes."

Not where I come from, it doesn't. Not yet, anyway. I can hear my mum's voice: "Girls get into trouble that way."

A girl in our class at school got pregnant, "in the family way", as people call it. She was in disgrace and she had to leave. I heard she went to some kind of home for unmarried mothers until the birth and had to give up the baby. It's a sad story that I know is true. So maybe "anything goes" for some people, but not for me. Luckily I don't find Baz at all attractive so Baz gets the push, and I move on to:

Philip:

Art school student. Black polo neck, black trousers, black socks and black underwear, I shouldn't wonder. He offers to sell me pot and I get confused. Why would I want to buy his old crockery? Kay steps in and says we won't be buying, thanks. I feel a right twit, a simple-minded out-of-towner, when she tells me that "pot" is an illegal drug. As Mr Kilter H. would say, I've still got a lot to learn.

The party is nearly over when we meet Barry Anovan, introduced as "the photographer". He's not as super-famous as David Bailey but he will be one day, according to Kay. He thinks that her willowy look is very "now" and asks if she would be interested in doing a photo shoot, so that he could show photos of her to magazines and get them both some work, hopefully.

"I'll certainly think about it, Barry, though I am pretty busy," says Kay, as cool as can be. "Now, have you met Jane Leachman and Percy Kilter, the top fashion stylists?" Percy and I look a little stunned, but we soon realise that Kay's introduction has worked, and Barry thinks we're already well-known. "The secret is to act as if you're 'it'," whispers Kay later. "This is the Sixties. You can be who you want to be!"

"Don't you want Barry to photograph you?" I ask.

"Of course I do! But I want him to think I'm already a hot fashion property. See. I'm being who I want to be!"

We dance the night away and leave the party as the sun rises, heading for a greasy spoon for a fry-up breakfast of bacon and eggs with steaming stripy mugs of tea.

Percy is fired up with excitement.

"You're right, Kay. We should be what we

want to be. So I've decided I'm going to make up some hipster flares and a trendy four-buttoned jacket, and I'm going to present them to Mrs Diggins from Plimptons. Are you with me, Jane? We could do it together."

"But what about your uncles? Shouldn't we ask them first?" I reply, anxiously.

"When the time is right," replies Percy evasively. "Let's make the samples first."

27 OCTOBER 1965

Norman tells me that the Beatles got their MBEs at Buckingham Palace. I relay the news to Mr Kilter B. in the shop and he is quite shocked by this.

"I thought you had to work for years in the Civil Service or save your battalion under fire to get a medal. But for singing pop records? What next?"

If only he knew! Hipster flares for Plimptons, that's what!

2 November 1965

We're working hard on the samples for Plimptons. They're boring things like navy jackets and tweed skirts. Meanwhile I'm also secretly helping Percy make a pair of hot purple velvet hipsters and a groovy jacket. Percy insists that until we're ready we should hide everything from his uncles, down to the last snippet of waste velvet. I am very worried about this, but Percy says it's vital we wait for the right time to tell them what we're doing.

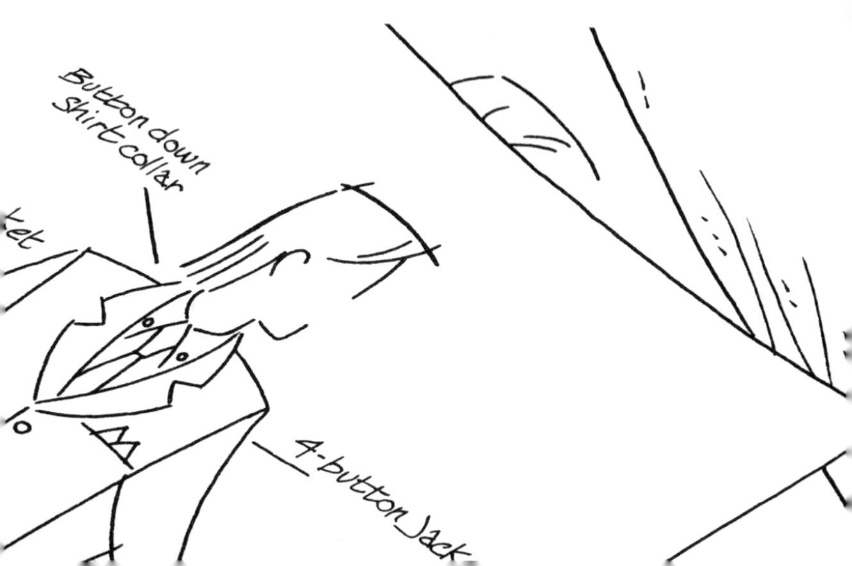

4 NOVEMBER 1965

D-DAY! It's time for the presentation to Mrs Diggins, buyer from Plimptons department store. Before she arrives Mr Kilter B. fills the front shop with flowers and we put the finishing touches to the sample garments – brushing and ironing them to perfection.

"Percy, have you asked your uncles if we can show the new outfit?" I hiss at Percy, who is looking shifty.

"No...I...I was going to last night but..."

"Percy!"

Just then Mr Kilter H. walks in, and thinks I look flustered because I'm nervous about Plimptons chief buyer.

"Don't worry, Jane. Mrs D. isn't a dragon. She's a pussycat after a few garibaldi biscuits and a cup of tea. The thing to remember about her is that she worships French couturier fashion. Ladies of her age do, you know."

"Percy, it's too late! We can't show the hipsters now! Not without asking!" I whisper, as Mrs Diggins arrives. She is ample and middle-aged, with a smart suit and a hairstyle that looks as stiff as concrete. The uncles turn into real charmers and move into action with garibaldis, tea and flattery. Trousers, skirts and jackets are held up and examined closely one by one.

"Thank you, Mr Kilters, both of you, and your young team. Up to your usual standard. There was a definite feel of Paris about it all."

"No higher praise, Mrs Diggins. Another garibaldi?"

"Oh, how kind. I'll take your clothing samples with me, of course, and let you know our requirements in due course."

It's all over, or so they think. Only Percy has disappeared into the back of the workshop, and before anyone can stop him he rushes back out carrying the new hipsters and jacket!

"No!" I squeak, but it's too late.

"Mrs Diggins. I'd like you to consider these for the new season."

The uncles stand stock still, showing no reaction. Mrs Diggins looks over the top of her glasses at Percy and speaks to him like a headmistress who has caught a schoolboy running in a corridor.

"Not Kilters' usual style, young man."

"No, but I think you'll find this 'London Look' is very popular," Percy offers.

Breathlessly I wondered – London? Not Paris? Will Mrs Diggins explode? Will the uncles chase us round with their dressmaking scissors? Will I be on the next train back to Coventry to spend the rest of my life on a factory line punching rivets into cars?

Well, Mrs Diggins gets up to leave without indicating what she thinks about the new gear. But I notice that a brief knowing look seems to pass between her and Mr Kilter H. The uncles stay super-smooth and put Percy's samples in with the rest. Percy and I wait fearfully out the back while they wave Mrs Diggins off.

"Why did you do that, Percy?" I hissed.

"I'm sorry. I just had to, Jane. I was too nervous to ask my uncles, and then it was too late, and then..."

The uncles came back inside. I was expecting their faces to look thunderous, but instead they looked almost amused.

"That went well, don't you think Henry?"

"Yes, I believe so, Benjamin. Garibaldi, Jane? There's one left."

"Do you think she likes the velvet stuff?" Percy blurts out.

"She might, my boy. She might," replies Mr Kilter B. "We won't hear for a while."

Mr Kilter H. winks at me and casually pulls out a piece of velvet hipster material that has been concealed in his pocket.

The old stager! He must have known all along we were making something with it!

"You're lucky Mrs Diggins is an old friend of ours, Percy. She was, shall we say, expecting something new today. You could have asked us, though. We're not that frightening, are we?"

"I'm sorry. Look, it wasn't Jane's fault..."

Percy stammers, but Mr H. puts a hand on his shoulder.

"Calm down, Percy. You both did well. Now let's see if she likes your ideas and then we'll talk about it."

7 November 1965

Still no news from Plimptons.

"Mrs Diggins is like a fine old vintage car. She will not be rushed," Mr Kilter H. assures us, but meanwhile I am really nervous and Percy can hardly sit still, he is so wound up. What if she hates the samples? What will we do then?

We need to relax a bit, so Kay and I find a funny quiz in one of our magazines titled, *Are You a Dollybird?* We try it out on Percy to cheer him up. It doesn't, but then he's *not* a dollybird!

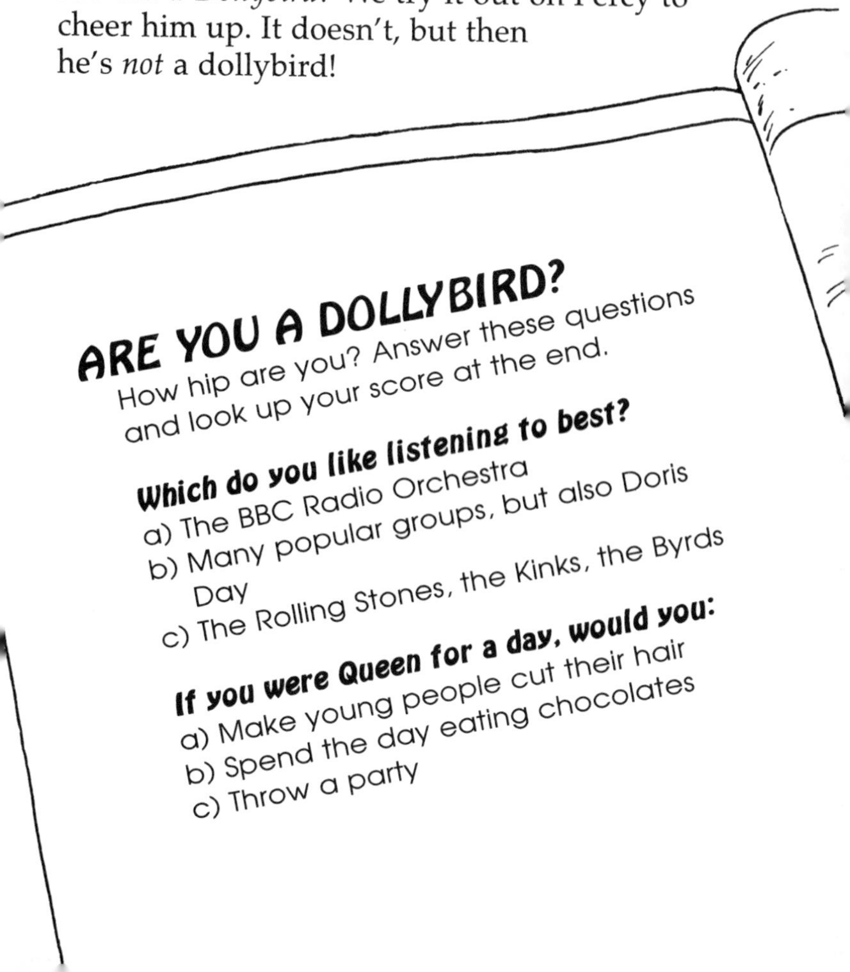

ARE YOU A DOLLYBIRD?

How hip are you? Answer these questions and look up your score at the end.

Which do you like listening to best?

a) The BBC Radio Orchestra
b) Many popular groups, but also Doris Day
c) The Rolling Stones, the Kinks, the Byrds

If you were Queen for a day, would you:

a) Make young people cut their hair
b) Spend the day eating chocolates
c) Throw a party

Where do you buy your clothes?

a) A draper's shop, which is also handy for knicker elastic and girdles
b) A 'club book' catalogue
c) A boutique

Which hero would you scream for at an airport?

a) The Prime Minister
b) The pilot
c) Paul McCartney

Your score:

Mostly a: You're so square you could be mistaken for your own parents. It's time to shake off the 1950s and get hip.

Mostly b: You'd like to be on the scene but your shoes are still too sensible. Try harder.

Mostly c: Yeah, baby!

You're hot!

5 December 1965

This morning Percy and I have our heads down, busy in the workshop, when Mr Kilter H. and Mr Kilter B. slip quietly in. One of them clears his throat, with an "I've got something important to say" cough. We stop what we're doing and for a few seconds it all goes deathly quiet.

I realise that Mrs Diggins has made her decision and it's hanging unspoken in the air between us. Then a smile breaks across both wrinkly old Kilter faces.

"Mrs Diggins liked it all, Percy," chuckles Mr Kilter H. "She's going to take our classic line but try a few of your modern items in a new part of the store set aside as a boutique, to be called Le Style Anglais I believe. Very far-sighted, our Mrs Diggins."

"Very," agrees Mr B., and they both laugh as I clap my hands and Percy blows out the breath he's been holding in.

"Now, Benjamin and I have been talking it over. You know we don't blame you for doing what you did at the presentation. We have left things the same around here for far too long, and haven't been fair to you. Now with Jane here, we realise we have not one, but two great fashion talents on our hands. We think that you two should concentrate on working up a small range that you might describe as 'with it'." Mr H. smiles at us both.

"But only if you both agree, of course,"adds Mr B.

"You mean our dream…Kilter Kit!"gasps Percy.

"Yes. Kilter Kit, if you like. That sounds like a good name. Mr H. and I will carry on making clothes for our more traditional clients, of course. But we realise that if you've got a dream it's no good sweeping it under the work table. It'll just pop right out again and make the place untidy until you use it."

So it's on! We're to design and make samples for a new fashion label, Kilter Kit. We both rush upstairs to tell Kay, whom we catch by surprise with her curlers on and her face plastered in beauty cream. We all dance around the formica-top table.

"We'll model the clothes on you, Kay! You'll be our muse, our inspiration," Percy cries. "Without the curlers, of course!"

8 December 1965

I join Percy and Kay to celebrate our good news in Luigi's, local Italian restaurant splendido, and the only place for miles around that will let women in wearing trousers or miniskirts.

Spaghetti bolognaise all round. How exotic my life is getting! The nearest we would get to this at home would be a tin of Heinz spaghetti in tomato sauce. Not bad on toast, but not exactly Venice in the moonlight.

Thinking about it, I decide that I am probably the first Leachman in centuries to eat in a restaurant since way back in the mists of history when some medieval Leachman gnawed pigs' bones in a tavern. I think restaurants could catch on with ordinary people in Britain, though when I told this theory to Norman recently he said that the chippie will always be better on account of getting a free newspaper wrapped around your dinner!

Percy warns that the bolognaise could have garlic in it and make our breath smell "foreign". This gives me an idea and I hatch a plan to spike a pork pie with garlic and give it to the foreigner-hating Mr Binton next time I visit home.

We go mad and order a bottle of wine (Percy calls it "vino collapso"). We are just toasting Mrs Diggins and the future of Kilter Kit when the odious Freddie Fortune, a.k.a. Bert Crump, sidles past, in an odious shiny suit. His matching shiny ears prick up.

"Kilter Kit? What's that? Some sort of camping gear for boy scouts?"

Percy can't keep quiet. "Actually it's our new range of up to the minute clothing."

"Up to the minute? Time has stood still for the Kilters since 1865. Have you tried winding your clock up, Perce?"

He is very full of himself and, uninvited, he sits down and pours himself a glass of wine.

"You should see my new collection. I call it Spacegirl. Space is all the rage, of course. Loads of astronauts swanning around up there. Everyone will be going on holiday to space come 1970, and they'll be wearing my clothes, no doubt. You must pop by the Emporium, Kay. We could do some photo shoots and show the pictures to the magazines. It could be just the right thing to launch your modelling career, dear. It's bound to be big." He swans off, carrying one of our glasses and leaving Percy as red as the vino.

"Space! Pah! It was all done last year. Do you remember that French collection – 'Moon Girl' it was called – silver boots and hats, that sort of thing. Bert is just copying. I don't know how he gets away with it. Kay, you won't do a photo shoot for him, will you?"

"No fear! I shan't try on his mouldy space rubbish. Your clothes will be miles better."

Then Kay leans forward and drops her voice like a James Bond spy.

"Now listen, you two. I've been invited to a Christmas Do in Chelsea. Achingly trendy. You must both come with me. I'll introduce you as a hot new design team, and you could make some good contacts." She flutters her false eyelashes, smiles her pale lipstick smile and the waiter immediately rushes over with more cheese.

17 December 1965

It's party time and we tog ourselves up as best we know how. Percy wears a natty shirt; Kay's in a little dress, go-go boots and amazingly big earrings that look like cheese triangles. I'm in a crochet number and I've painted spots on my shoes because they're all the rage. I can wipe them off next week if they go out of fashion.

"All for one and one for all!" says Jane, when we're ready to go. "Between us we look the bees' knees!"

We travel across to Chelsea and into the most way-out flat I've ever seen – all velvet hangings and eastern lamps. People are lolling round on the floor on piles of giant cushions, smoking something that's definitely not from Dad's old tobacco tin.

Coloured lights slide over the walls and ceiling in oily patterns. The latest Kinks' music floats through the perfumed air…but I like the lovely toilet best. We lasses from north of Watford are

dead impressed by a lav that has art on the walls! Who'd have thought a loo could be cool.

We are introduced to the host, one Louis LeBrun, "kinetic sculptor" and all-round arty type. He is with his German girlfriend, Helga. It is all very hip and I begin to feel nervous. What will they make of a red-haired girl from Coventry?

"Be what you want to be," whispers Kay, and introduces me as "the fashion designer Jane Leachman" to a very posh young man called Nigel Greenington, who's been to Oxford University. No one I know from home has ever got to university.

Percy rushes over, very excited.

"These are the people we need to wear our clothes!" he gushes and starts telling Helga, Louis and Nigel how fab Kilter Kit is going to be. Louis waves his arms artistically in reply.

"You are a creative, Percy. Creativity is all."

"Have you travelled? Air travel is wonderful; so creative," Helga turns to me and I instantly feel a right Charlie. I've never been abroad and don't know anyone who has. I've been on camping holidays with Mum and Dad but guess that Helga might not be expecting stories about picnics eaten in the car because it's raining.

Luckily Nigel interrupts. "You Kilter Kit chappies sound as if you need to see my cousin, Daphne Worth."

"You mean Daphne Worth, the fashion editor of *Exclusive* magazine?" replies Kay, sounding surprised.

"Yes, that's the filly. I could get you an introduction if you like. She might do a feature on your clothes, if she likes them."

Nigel, Nigel, Nigel! We love you!

We get a lift home in the lovable Nigel's Triumph Herald, laughing and waving at the morning milkman like starlets in a movie.

I can tick two boxes on my chart of life's experiences today. For the first time I've met someone from Oxford University, and someone who's been in an aeroplane. Three boxes if you count meeting a "kinetic sculptor"!

2 January 1966

I come back to London on the train after Christmas. It takes about as long as going across Africa (or feels that way). The passengers spend their time smoking, coughing and eating luncheon meat and Branston pickle butties (or, if they're unlucky, fish paste). I sit thinking about how things have changed for me in the past year. My old life in Coventry seems far, far behind me.

Still, I had a good time at Mum and Dad's over Christmas. Dave has changed his image and is trying to look like a member of the Rolling Stones. Mum isn't happy about this because she feels they've got "something satanic" about them, but Dad tells her not to be so daft – "They're just young lads trying to make a few bob before they get proper jobs."

Our horrible neighbour Mr Binton appears on Boxing Day and I put my plan into action by offering him a garlic-spiked pork pie. Disappointingly he refuses to eat it because he says it smells off, but he puts it in his pocket and I get partial victory later when I see his nasty dog chewing it in the back garden.

Mum and Dad gave me a little transistor radio so I can listen to pirate radio stations when I'm in bed at night. Gran gave me a groovy plastic handbag with a handle made of fake daisies. Dave gave me a cushion cover printed with a picture of the Beatles on it, which left Mum fretting: "Will it wash all right?"

My presents now safely packed in my suitcase, I watch as back yards and brick terraces rush past the rain-smeared train window, and I realise with surprise that now London really feels like my home.

5 January 1966

New Year, new style! Percy and I are working really hard on the Kilter Kit stuff and the workshop is knee deep in brightly-coloured fabric and pattern pieces. The tailors' dummies are fitted up with dandy-looking jackets in a kind of Sixties-meets-Edwardian style. We've done some girl's clothes, too – blouses and mini pinafores. I love them.

9 JANUARY 1966

The lovable Nigel has come through on his promise and Daphne Worth, super-cool fashion editor at *Exclusive*, says she might meet us and do an article. This could be our big break! But first she wants to see some photos of our stuff, so Kay speaks to Barry Anovan, the photographer she met at the party up the road, and fixes a session in his studio tomorrow. She is going to model the girls' clothes for the photo shoot, and the men's clothes are going to go on one of our tailors' dummies. (We tried to persuade Percy to model but he was too shy. He said he'd wear a Kilter Kit outfit to the *Exclusive* meeting, though.)

I'm in charge of the styling, so I've been frantically collecting dangly earrings, long bead necklaces, scarves and hairbands.

Mr H. offers me a few of his old cravats, which will look fantastic with the men's shirts. "I wore these as a young man. Funny how style comes around, if you live long enough," he smiles. Will I have children who will want to wear my old miniskirts in twenty years' time, I wonder? One of the cravats has tiny Ks all over it.

"Short for Kilter, of course. I hope it brings you luck," says Mr H. When all the clothes are ready the uncles surprise us in the workshop with a bottle of bubbly.

"Here's to the success of Kilter Kit! We are very impressed with the collection, aren't we, Mr B.?"

"Absolutely, Mr H. I think one might describe it as groovy!"

9 JANUARY 1966

The day starts early with a trip to Mr Montelle, ace local coiffeur (hairdresser to the rest of us). He gives Kay a really stylish short geometric cut. Then he turns to Percy and me.

"Who's next?"

"We're not modelling," splutters Percy.

"No, but you're fashion designers, aren't you? You've got to look the part."

He eyes my red hair, the bane of my life. A colour not fashionable since Boudicca, it brought the nickname "carrot top" to the mind of every other schoolkid I ever met.

In a flash I find myself sitting in the hairdresser's chair. Mr Montelle's scissors work like lightning and soon my hair is short at the back, longer at the front.

"The Lulu," Mr Montelle calls it.

I look at myself in the mirror, and smile in wonder as a sophisticated-looking girl about town smiles back at me! Percy gets his hair tamed into a smooth "Cliff Richard"style. Then Mr Montelle puts enough hairspray on to leave our new hairdos hurricane and earthquake-proof and, loaded up with our precious collection, we make our way to Barry Anovan's photography studio.

We arrive down a Soho back street at what looks like an old warehouse.

"Are we lost?" Percy asks.

"No, we're not. We've just arrived at the centre of the swinging world," laughs Kay, pushing open the red-painted door.

Inside the walls are white, and lined with giant black and white pictures of blown-up objects. From the end of the corridor we can hear some kind of super-cool dance music. Through another door we reach an all white room. There are lights everywhere, big and small, on stands or fixed to the ceiling. Large rolls of white paper hang down from rollers on the walls.

"Ciao," Barry welcomes us in. "Love the tailor's dummy. OK, lets get cooking." He has an

assistant called Keith who doesn't say a single word except "Righto."

Barry and Keith spend an age moving lights around while Percy and I get Kay ready with black eyeliner and super-long false eyelashes. Then Barry puts on some jazz and pulls down a roll of the white paper for Kay to stand on, as a plain background.

"OK, I want you to start by dancing, posing, doing what you feel like. I'll keep taking the pictures." Kay seems to come to life for his camera instantly.

"Good! Move to the music. Feel the vibes. Come on, show me how to groove it!" Barry goes on like this and it works because Kay seems to light up and perform as if she'd been born in a photography studio.

"OK!" Click, click.

"Show me! Show me!" Click.

"You're beautiful! Yeah!" Click, click.

"Let's take a break. Cups of tea all round, Keith."

"Righto."

It all takes an age and is very tiring. There are constant lighting changes, new poses to try, outfit changes, accessory swops...Kay dances, sits on a bar stool, lies on the floor, jumps in the air, and looks fabulous throughout. Barry seems to take a million pictures but says that when he's developed the films and looked at them all, only about ten will be perfect.

"How will you choose them?" I ask.

"Oh, a gut feeling. There'll be a couple with atmosphere, a couple that instantly say 1966, and hopefully there will be one or two that really take your breath away."

13 January 1966

Norman's got news for me:

"It says on page one that Mrs Gandhi has become India's Prime Minister. Just imagine, a woman PM. Mind you, my missus has been in charge of me for years.

You'll be interested in the centre pages, Jane. They're all about miniskirts. Some people think they're evil, apparently. It says here that women can smoke, drink, swear and take the pill. But will the miniskirt corrupt them?"

"What a load of rubbish!" I reply.

"Whoa there! I don't write the stuff. I just sell it. Maybe you should make my missus one of those miniskirts, Jane!"

In fact I hardly have time for any work because Barry's photos arrive today, looking fabulous.

I get the job of taking them by taxi straight round to the *Exclusive* offices which are in a large important-looking building in the West End. I go in nervously and give the packet of labelled photos to the receptionist, who just looks at me coolly.

"Er, these are for Daphne Worth, thank you," I mutter, and scuttle out feeling terrified!

16 January 1966

A handwritten note arrives in the post from *Exclusive*.

Loved the piccies. Bring the clothes over to show me after New Year, when I get back from my ski party in Monaco. We only feature quality work, so I need to see the seams.

Regards, Daphne Worth.

No problem there. Our seams are perfect, thanks to the excellent training the Kilter uncles have given us. So, in a couple of weeks' time we'll get our biggest chance of success so far!

22 January 1966

My wish list for 1966

Nasty neighbour Mr Binton discovers he likes Bob Dylan records, curry and eastern philosophy. He moves to Kashmir, taking Mrs Binton with him.

Kay meets the Beatles in the greengrocer. Ringo, George and John fight each other for the right to propose to her. I get Paul.

England wins the World Cup.

New inventions mean the train to Coventry is fitted with super-fast hover jets and passengers are given anti train-wobble pills.

Percy and I get MBEs for our contribution to fashion.

A girl can dream!

3 February 1966

We're busy in the workshop when a nasty smell of cheap aftershave fills the air, followed by the shape of Freddie Fortune (a.k.a. Bert Crump) appearing at the back door. He's timed his visit so that Mr B. and Mr H. are out having their usual tea break.

"Morning, pussycats. I heard you were busy," he sneers.

Percy grabs the photos of Kay in Kilter Kit and shoves them into a drawer. I grab the material samples and stuff them in my pockets, so that everything important will be hidden. But Freddie picks up a snippet off the floor.

"Velvet again? Bit last week, don't you think? What are you up to, then? Making a job-lot of fancy dress?"

He knows just how to wind Percy up "like a good 'un," as Dad would say, and, sure enough, Percy lets the cat straight out of the bag.

"Actually we're getting ready for a meeting with *Exclusive*. We're very busy, so if you've nothing pressing to say, we must get on."

"All right, all right. Keep your hair on, Perce old son." Freddie's eyes sweep over the workshop, and then he turns to leave.

"Toodle-oo, then. I must get back to my emporium. There's no rest for the successful designer."

"You should get plenty of time off, then," mutters Percy as Freddie disappears off up the street, whistling tunelessly.

7 February 1966

We are getting very jumpy as the meeting comes nearer. For instance, this morning when we arrive at the workshop, the back door is mysteriously open.

"We've been burgled!" cries Percy and we rush inside, expecting the worst. But everything looked just the same, and it seems Percy just forgot to lock up last night. Thank heavens the meeting is tomorrow as I think he's beginning to crack up with the strain of waiting, and I'm not far behind! Just a few more hours to go.

9 February 1966

Today was the day of the fateful meeting at *Exclusive*, and by rights tomorrow's newspapers ought to read: *Kilter Kit in Total Utter Titanic-style Disaster*. It's so painful to write about, but as self-appointed historian of the Sixties I can't shirk my duty, so here goes:

Percy and I start well enough, arriving early with our samples at the magazine offices. We've tried extra hard with our appearance, knowing that Daphne Worth will probably be dressed in the most super-stylish outfit in the world. Percy is wearing some velvet trousers from our collection and I'm in one of the pinafores so we look the part, even though I think we're both feeling pretty terrified. The receptionist glances at us expresssionlessly and tells us to wait in the foyer, where the walls are lined with framed magazine covers showing the hippest of the hip. Beautiful people waft past. Was that Elizabeth Taylor? Richard Burton? No, it's the tea lady and the postman, but everyone looks like a star around here. Well, everyone except us.

Eventually an assistant called Babs floats down and leads us into the presence of style dragon Daphne Worth, who is wearing big black and white op-art glasses like some sort of fashion owl.

"Loved your snaps. Barry is hot, isn't he? And that model you used. What's her name? I like her style. Babs, would you get coffee, darling?

I'm interested in doing a feature on your clothes but I need to know they're well made. We only feature quality you see. As I always say, our readers are "the creme de la", darlings. They don't want clothes that fall apart at dinner."

She starts to unfold the samples. "Where are you selling? Who are your main buyers? Do you have anyone famous wearing your clothes yet?"

"Er, well, we've got a couple of outfits in Plimptons..." This answer sounds pretty pathetic.

"Well, you've got some way to go before you make it into the Mary Quant league, haven't you? But things happen overnight these days. You could be the next big thing, especially if we do you in the magazine."

She is looking closely at the goods. This seems like plain sailing so far...

"Mmm. Nice choice of fabric. But are they made well?"

At just that moment, Babs comes in carrying a tray of Union Jack coffee mugs. Daphne picks up a sugar spoon and it slips through her manicured fingers on to the floor. Percy sees a chance for gallantry.

"I'll get it," he cries and bends over, accompanied by a ripping noise as cloth tears apart. He freezes mid-bend and looks round startled. His trousers have split to reveal a pair of underpants printed with a picture of pop star Cilla Black.

"Good Lord!" Daphne gasps, her thin, pencilled eyebrows shooting up. "I can't feature clothes that split at the slightest strain!" Before she gets a chance to say another word we grab our samples and rush out of there past an open-mouthed Babs.

The icy receptionist in the foyer doesn't even say goodbye as we hurry into the street outside, where the winter wind blows away the tears running down my cheeks.

"That's it!" wails Percy. "That's it. Failure!"

10 February 1966

Percy and I are in mourning for Kilter Kit. Our big chance seems to be over, although Kay is trying to persuade us to try again.

"*Exclusive* isn't everything. You can find a new way to launch Kilter Kit. You don't need Daphne Worth to tell you whether you're good or not."

"Well, we're not, are we? Our bloody seams split."

I've been thinking about it all night. What went wrong? That faulty trouser seam is a mystery. I know we double-sewed all those seams and double-checked them too.

Later on in the day I get a big clue to the mystery. I'm back in the flat doing my washing in the bath when the doorbell rings and Kay answers it to that greaseball Freddie Fortune.

"Ciao, pussycat." He bounds up the stairs to the living room, as oily as a car-mechanic's vest. Evidently he thinks Kay is home alone, so I keep quiet and listen to what he says.

"So, I heard that Percy split a bit!" He snorts

with laughter. "This Kilter Kit business is finished. Ditch them, Kay. Come and model my gear instead. I'm getting a new good collection ready, my best yet. I'm going to take it to *Exclusive*".

"How original of you," Kay sniffs. "But frankly, Freddie, I certainly wouldn't trust your seams."

"Oh, I see. It's like that is it? Bit of a crush on old Perce, have we? Wrong choice, darling. He's a loser. I know because I worked at Kilter's once."

I hear Kay walk out of the room, and then Freddie muttering privately to himself as he leaves: "And I've still got a key. As for seams, I may not sew 'em strong but I know how to unpick one double-quick."

I think I'm beginning to see what happened, though I can't prove it. I reckon Freddie used his old key to get into our workshop and sabotage the seam on Percy's trousers. I'll bet he had a good snoop round our collection and set of photos, too...

I won't tell Percy about my theory yet. After all I can't prove it. No, a bit more detective work is needed...

4 March 1966

All our hard work, and then the meeting disaster has left me feeling tired. Mr B. and Mr H. said I should have a few days off, and that's why I'm writing this on a rickety train – dirty and bone-jarringly wobbly, but taking me back to Mum and Dad.

I've left poor old Percy long-faced and slumped over his work table, as if the world is officially going to end and there's nothing to be done; we'll all just have to lump it. He says at the moment he feels like giving up with Kilter Kit.

I haven't told him my suspicions about Freddie (in case he goes off the deep end) but I have confided in Kay, who is really angry and is as determined as I am to prove Freddie guilty.

My break at home will give me a chance to think it all through.

I can tell the train is getting close to Coventry because I can see factories on the skyline.

Clackety clack. Clackety clack.

Next stop Coventry!

5 March 1966

With just one train trip I seem to have slithered straight back to childhood and landed on my soft bed in my little room at home, with my dolls and my old Enid Blyton books. Some things have changed, though. Dave has formed a band with his friends. They've played a few dates at local halls, doing versions of the latest pop songs, and I hope I'll be able to see them at it before I go back to London. They've called themselves the Hot Potatoes. Well, it's no sillier than the Beatles, I'd say.

I can hear Mum downstairs cooking tea (sausages and rice pud). How come we leave all the cooking and cleaning to Mum in this house? We're as likely to see a unicorn as Dad helping in the kitchen. Dave and I have been the same up to now, even though they say our generation is going to change all that "the little woman stays at home" stuff. Well, now I live in my own place I realise what hard work it all is. I definitely think it's time for change in the Leachman household. Dad doesn't seem to have come to the same conclusion, and is lying on the sofa reading the paper.

"Have you seen this model, Twiggy she's called? They're calling her the 'Face of Sixty-Six'. She's as thin as a stick. Needs a good meal. Ma, is tea ready yet?"

6 March 1966

Last night I challenged Dad to cook tea for us today. Mum went quiet and looked as if I'd suggested he run round Coventry city centre in the buff.

"I could, you know. We did cooking in the army during National Service. Kettle-boiling by numbers," jokes Dad.

"Go on then, cook for us!" I challenge him. "It's the Sixties now. Men are going to have to start pulling their weight around the house because us women will be busy, won't we, Mum?"

"All right, you're on!" agrees Dad.

So this evening he is installed behind the kitchen door, firmly shut and guarded by Dave and me, to stop Mum going in and taking over.

Suspiciously, we hear the sound of a newspaper turning...But he must be doing something in there because good smells are wafting out. At last he appears in a pinny, carrying what can only be described as a triumph, a steaming golden-crusted pie. It looks good. It smells fantastic. Hold on. There's no washing up... No dirty pots and pans. Evidence of cheating, I'd say!

At last he admits it. "You know that greengrocer's shop round the corner? It's been done out as a supermarket. Loads of new stuff, it's got. You can even buy food from a freezer.

Hard as a brick it is, until it thaws out. Oh yes. We're up to date in Coventry, we are! Soon you might not need to cook at all, Eileen. We'll all be sucking food out of tubes, like astronauts."

7 March 1966

Mr Binton sticks his head over the fence to complain about Dave's guitar practice. He sees my new haircut and is predictably rude.

"Do you go out like that?"

"Yes, actually. I'm going to see the Hot Potatoes tonight at the Palais. Get with it, Mr Binton!"

I go shopping downtown to find a new outfit and bump into Doreen, who was at school with me. She's married with a baby now, and she's moved into one of the new tower blocks they're building. "It's lovely. Ever so modern; all concrete and that. Electric fires, so we don't need the coalman to call, and there's no garden to be bothered with."

As far as she's concerned I'm as weird as a Martian because I'm not interested in husbands or babies yet. It makes me realise that though people say the Sixties are new and different, there's still a long way to go before ideas change around here.

8 March 1966

Dave and the boys play brilliantly at the Palais and they get everyone dancing. But to my eye they could do with a new look. Nowadays pop groups dress in one style – the Beatles have suits, the Beach Boys have white trousers, but the Hot Potatoes are all over the place. They need some groovy threads.

Aha, I feel a plan coming on!

9 March 1966

A red letter day for the Leachmans!

After the show a talent scout comes up to Dave and offers the group a spot on TV in a talent contest. It could be their big break, and with one bound I jump on the bandwagon and offer my help in the shape of Kilter Kit. The group will be coming to London for the show so I suggest that Percy and I design and make some outfits for them. That way they'll look the part, Kilter Kit will be shown on TV, and when they become stars (as I'm sure they will) Percy and I will be hanging on to their superstar coat-tails.

Dave and the boys think it's a cool scheme and I rush to the nearest phone box to ring Percy. As usual there's a queue and I can't help hopping excitedly from foot to foot while I wait my turn.

"Aren't you a bit cold, love?" asks the man in front. "Whoever thought up the miniskirt didn't take into account an east wind in March, did they?" He's right, but sometimes you have to suffer for fashion.

Percy is excited by my idea.

"It'll put Kilter Kit back in the spotlight. Jane, you're brilliant!"

In this case I think I agree.

2 April 1966

I'm back in lively London, always bubbling up with something new. This week, according to the London papers, we should all have our hair cut in a fringe and be seen at the Beat Club in Soho. Meanwhile Labour have won the general election again and World Cup fever is everywhere, because it's going to held at Wembley soon. Will England win the cup?

Meanwhile will Kilter Kit roar back from disaster to triumph? In the workshop we start planning our top-secret mission – the creation of the Hot Potatoes look. We start by visiting Carnaby Street, chock-full of boutiques where the fashion pulse beats strongest. We come back with our heads buzzing with ideas, and we get sketching.

Mr H. makes a good point, that TV programmes are black and white, and we need to take that into account in our designs. So strong black and white patterns become the theme.

Top-secret
sketches!

Vents at back
of jacket

Double breast
tailored look

2B

Union Jacks
painted on Boots

Hipster waist
illed shirt cuffs
Flare from the knee

10 April 1966

We go to Luigi's for supper and find Freddie Fortune holding court at our usual table. He pretends not to notice us but starts talking very loudly so we can hear.

"Luigi, love. Your finest bottle of vino, if you please. I'm celebrating. My collection is ready for *Exclusive* to see. They're going to flip over my new ideas."

Kay and I look at each other. It's time us girls took action.

27 April 1966

Kay has entered the lion's den, Freddie Fortune's Gear Emporium. She pretended to be fed up with me and Percy, and told him she might be interested in modelling his stuff. A delighted Freddie believed her and showed her what he'd made to show *Exclusive*.

She came home white-faced.

"I couldn't believe it, Jane! He's copied your collection completely! He's got pinafores and Edwardian velvet suits, the lot! He's taking them to show Daphne Worth. It's not fair! He's a thief!"

"What if we tell Daphne? We can't prove he copied us. She'd probably think we were just lying," I reply.

"Ah, but I think we can prove it. Do you remember Mr H. lent you some of his old cravats for the photos that Barry took? One of them was very distinctive, wasn't it? I remember, it had lots of little Ks on it. Well, Freddie's got it. I saw it right there in amongst his stuff. He must have taken it from your workshop!"

"Kay, that's it! The proof we need! That exact same cravat appeared on our photos and it's unique - a one-off original that Mr H. made himself. Now we can stop Freddie in his tracks!"

28 April 1966

Today I conquered my nerves, steeled myself to succeed and went back to the offices of *Exclusive*.

"Be what you want to be," I kept saying to myself as I walked proudly past the hard-faced receptionist and up the stairs to Daphne Worth's office.

She and I had a good talk, and I think she found it very interesting...

5 May 1966

Today a group of plumbers arrive at the workshop door, carrying toolbags and wearing overalls.

"All right, our Jane?" asks one, and I realise that it is none other than Dave and the Hot Potatoes, all the way from deepest darkest Coventry.

"You said you were hiding everything from this Freddie Fortune bloke, so we've come in disguise. That way he'll think we're plumbers, not a pop group!"

They each have a fitting for the outfits they're going to wear on the TV talent contest.

"We're gonna look like the business, we are. We'll 'ave girls all over us, like."

"Eh, what if they rip our clothes off? Fans do that sometimes, you know. What sort of underwear should we have on?"

The group have decided they need a manager, and it so happens we know just the man, none other than top toff Nigel Greenington from Eton and Oxford University. He has dipped his elegant fingers into several pies and started managing pop groups. He arrives in big style at the workshop to meet the Hots, driving his new wheels, a van decorated in bright swirling colours by kinetic artist Louis.

"I call it the Love Machine. Gotta look the part, Jane. That's what it's all about these days. Why have you got the plumbers in?"

His accent has subtly changed and now he sounds less like a BBC announcer and more like Mick Jagger. He seems to get on well with the lads and whisks them off to Carnaby Street to meet some beautiful people and do some publicity photos. At the end of the day they go back to Coventry happy and we can get back to work on their special TV outfits.

10 May 1966

London is swinging, according to an American magazine, and the word has caught on, especially with Percy who is convinced that we are personally helping to get the swing going.

"I like that word 'swinging'," says Mr B. "The 1920s were 'roaring', they used to say, and the 1890s were always described as 'naughty'. I wonder what we'll be doing in the 1970s?"

"Eating space food, apparently," I suggest.

"Driving cars that can fly, and wearing glasses that can play movies in front of our eyes," replies Percy. "And we'll be wearing jet packs in our shoes. By the year 2000 we'll have them fitted into our bodies."

"Yuck!"

"No, it'll be great. I can't wait! We won't need cars any more."

"Hold on. What will people do in Coventry if they can't build cars?"

"Oh well. They probably won't need to work at all."

We get a big surprise when Mr H. walks in with none other than Mrs Diggins, Plimpton's buyer, on his arm.

"Your things have sold very well in our new boutique, my dears. Keep it up. Mr H. has been telling me about your television plans, too. If I can help, let me know. The loan of some accessories, perhaps? We like to help the new generation, don't we, Henry?" She pats Mr H.'s hand and continues. "You might like to know I saw Freddie Fortune. Odious man. Offered me stale bourbons, and a couple of badly-made pinafores. A little bird, I won't say who, has let me know that he's in the habit of copying better designers' ideas. Well he's certainly not welcome at Plimptons any more!"

Good old Mrs D! And good old Daphne! But will Freddie be out to get revenge on me now, I wonder?

15 May 1966

We see Mick Jagger from the Rolling Stones walking past the window of Luigi's. Kay says it is an omen. "The beautiful people are coming to NW6, drawn here by an invisible style magnet."

As Mick Jagger walks down the street he causes a stir, and the news soon reaches Freddie Fortune, who comes running along the pavement to find him, no doubt drooling at the thought of meeting a famous person. Meanwhile Mick has climbed into a shiny limousine and disappeared, the invisible style magnet having presumably been turned off.

"Where has he gone?" Freddie mouths through the window at us. We make faces back at him. I hate that man!

"When we're famous we'll know Mick," Kay announces. "He'll come for tea, a plate of beans on toast at our place...And we'll have to tidy our wet washing away. Hmm, maybe we won't invite him after all."

18 May 1966

Nigel pops by to show us some publicity pictures he took when the Hot Potatoes were in town. They're walking down Carnaby Street or larking about in front of the boutiques. They look OK now, but they'll look really cool when they get their new Kilter Kit on.

GEAR
RNABY ST
FAB
37
FAB
FAB
FAB

GEA
34 L

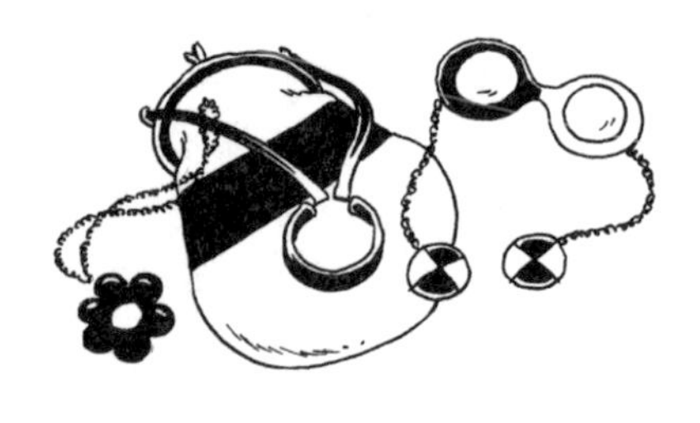

10 JUNE 1966

Tomorrow is the big day – the TV appearance of the Hot Potatoes in Kilter Kit. They have arrived hotfoot from Coventry and tonight they are all squashed into our flat, sleeping on the floor or the furniture.

"Hey, Jane. Can you move this wet washing?"

"Have you got any more beans on toast?"

Their equipment is outside in Nigel's Love Machine, which is being closely guarded by the eagle eyes of Luigi from his restaurant window. Thank goodness it's dark and nosy Freddie Fortune won't notice a freaky-looking vehicle parked suspiciously near the workshop. We don't want anything to go wrong now, and he *is* trouble.

The Hot Potato boys are due at the television studio first thing in the morning so today we take them over to Mr Montelle's for a trim, and try not to giggle when we see them sitting in a row under the hairdryers. Their hairstyles are ready. Their clothes are ready. Their song is ready. But is the world ready? Roll on tomorrow.

I can hear the group talking downstairs. They're obviously nervous, even though they've played lots of dates in front of audiences before.

"It's the TV, though. It's different. They'll be swinging those great big cameras all around us with men sitting on the back. What if we mess up?"

"It won't matter. It's not going out live. We can just do it again."

"That makes it worse. We're bound to mess it up now you've said that."

"Shut up, will ya. Let's get some kip. And mind you don't mess up your hair."

11 June 1966

Morning

The boys look as good as we can make them and Nigel drives them off in the Love Machine. Each one has a shirt with long frilled cuffs that stick out from beneath the sleeves of a boldly striped Edwardian jacket. Their trousers are tight at the top (with extra-strong seams), and flared at the bottom, with Union Jack boots.

Dave gives me a hug.

"We look the business, Jane. Thanks."

"It was a pleasure, Dave. Now the rest is up to you."

We wave them off, and as they disappear round the corner Freddie Fortune comes bounding along, too late to discover our secret.

"I heard there was some sort of painted bus blocking the pavement. Are you selling ice creams to make a few bob, Percy?"

Percy is about to open his mouth and blab, but I stand on his toes and he yelps instead.

"I'm off. Can't waste time here," Freddie smirks. "I'm presenting a whole new collection to the lovely Daphne Worth today. You know her, don't you? I'll be sure to let her know about your new ice-cream venture."

Evening

The boys still aren't back yet, and it's late by now. We're trying to keep awake with mug after mug of coffee. We've no idea how they got on today.

"Maybe it was a disaster and they've gone off home to Coventry," I fret.

"Nigel has probably taken them partying," Kay suggests.

Hold on...I can hear the engine of an old van outside and the strains of someone singing: "Yeah, yeah, yeah! She loves you, yeah, yeah, yeah!"

They're back!

14 JUNE 1966

It's a bit late at night to be writing in a diary, but I can't sleep, and anyway it's my solemn duty as an official historian of the 1960s to announce...

A huge success!

The time of our triumph? This evening at eight p.m. The scene of our triumph – Luigi's restaurant, where everyone gathers round a TV to see the appearance of the Hot Potatoes. Kay, Percy and I sit nervously picking wax off the candleholders. Mr B., Mr H., Norman, Luigi, and the whole street seem to be there, except for Freddie.

No-one seems to have seen him for days.

At last the programme comes on and the cameras show lots of trendy young girls dancing to the theme tune in their minis, hairbands and twirling beads.

Because it is a talent contest we have to sit through an opera singer, a man with performing parrots and a spoon player before the presenter finally announces: "And now a brand new group from Coventry, looking very groovy tonight and ready to raise the roof. Ladies and gentlemen, give a warm welcome to THE HOT POTATOES!"

Suddenly there they are on screen, looking fantastic in their Kilter Kit, launching into their new song "Hung Up On You".

"I'm hung up on you, babe.
Thought you'd be true, babe.
What can I do, babe!"
3

At the end the studio audience give them a rapturous reception.

"Their playing was hot and their clothes were hot, ladies and gentlemen. Will you vote for the Hot Potatoes tonight?" The votes for all the contestants get shown on some kind of rickety-looking machine, and its arrow goes haywire for the Hot Potatoes.

Kay and I squeal and hug each other. Percy punches the air: "Yes!"

Mr B. and Mr H. hug everyone!

They won!
We won!

Thunderbirds are go!

8 JULY 1966

It's party time again, only this time it's in our flat, so, of course, the party scores will be perfect. The records are ready on the turntable. The nibbles are out on plates and all the washing has been bundled away. Our guests of honour will be the Hot Potatoes, men of the moment after their TV triumph and fresh from lots of press interviews, during which they mentioned Kilter Kit as often as possible (I told them to, anyway).

Norman has some publicity news.

"Well done to your brother and his group, Jane! They're really making a splash. The papers are full of the World Cup but they've still made room for a mention of the Hot Potatoes. Look, there's a photo on page three. 'The new pop sensation from Coventry,' it says. They look good in those suits."

9 JULY 1966

The Party Report, by Jane Leachman, from now on to be known as the perfect hostess.

Clothes 10, Food 10, Everything 10.

Guests include the Kilters, H. and B., Percy, Nigel, the Hots and everyone else we know. The flat fills to bursting point.

I meet Adam, the politically-minded man I've spoken to before. He says that he's given up trying to start a revolution and is about to travel round India looking for "answers to life".

"I want to catch the spirit of freedom, man. It's blowin' in the wind, you know."

Baz, the man who once suggested we "let it all hang out" together, arrives with his new fiancé, a librarian from Staines. Philip the grass-dealing art student is technically at the party, but so stoned he could be on another planet.

The only person who doesn't put in an appearance is Freddie Fortune.

"Where is that creep?" asks Percy. "He normally gatecrashes everything going."

"Well, it's like this, Percy..." I sit him down and explain how Freddie broke into the workshop and unpicked the trouser seam.

"I'll kill him!" Percy cries.

"Calm down. There's no need." I go on to

explain how we discovered the evidence of the cravat.

"I went to see Daphne Worth and explained it all to her. She said that Freddie would never get into her magazine and she would make sure everyone important in fashion knew about his behaviour. She sent him packing, but says she's still dead interested in us and definitely wants to do an article on us and Kilter Kit. She says that now we've really arrived!"

20 July 1966

Freddie Fortune has been sighted. According to Norman he is changing his name to Darius Starlight and is moving to Muswell Hill. I've been half expecting to see him in the chippie, but now he's gone for good. Who knows where he'll end up...

30 July 1966

The country goes wild, and here's why:

England are playing West Germany in the World Cup Final. The referee blows his whistle for the end of ninety minutes and it's still a draw at 2-2. The tension is almost unbearable. There's going to be extra time.

Geoff Hurst gets the ball. He controls it; twists his body; shoots...It hits the bar of the German goal! It bounces out! Did it go over the line? The referee says yes! It's a goal! England are on top of the world, and Hurst becomes a god, there and then.

The clock ticks down; there are seconds to go, when Hurst uses his godlike powers to score again!

"They think it's all over. It is now!" With the commentator's words England starts to celebrate. We go up to the West End, and end up dancing in Trafalgar Square. We won, we won!

31 July 1966

The newspapers are full of pictures of the World Cup team, and Percy has a dangerous gleam in his eye. Heads down, everybody. He's got another crazy scheme.

"I've got a plan, Jane. A new dream! Imagine if we could get those England football stars to wear Kilter Kit. All we need to do is to get their measurements, make up some clothes, meet them, hand them the stuff for free…I can see Nobby Stiles in hipsters with a peaked cap, and Bobby Moore in a brocade jacket, and Geoff Hurst in purple…"

Here we go again. As we haven't got enough to do already! Pass the pencil, will you? Our country needs us!

Exclusive Magazine August 1966

SHORT AND SWEET

Kilter Kit is a new fashion label that's really going places, thanks to Coventry group the Hot Potatoes. They wore groovy Kilter gear for the launch of their new hit single "**Hung Up On You**". Now everyone wants the Kilter label in their wardrobe.

Designers Jane Leachman and Percy Kilter have caught the mood of swinging London with their Edwardian-style men's jackets, tight-fitting hipsters and oh so romantic shirts. For women there are adorable mini pinafores, to be teamed with white tights and hairbands for that beat-baby look.

Any couple wearing Kilter Kit will be hot this season!

THE WORLD OF THE SIXTIES

Here is some extra background for keen history hunters.

1960s ISSUES

Here are some of the issues people would have discussed in the 1960s:

"THE PERMISSIVE SOCIETY"

People argued about morality, such as whether people should have sex before marriage. It was extremely unusual for couples to live together without marrying. Books, plays, magazines and films were banned altogether if they were thought to be too rude or violent.

DRUGS

Drugs were in the news. Stars such as the Beatles were arrested for having pot or grass (nicknames for marijuana), and this shocked many people. In the late 1960s drugs were a common subject in art and pop music.

WOMEN'S RIGHTS

It was very unusual for women to reach top positions in business or government, because many still gave up work when they married and had a family. But in the 1960s women's rights became a bigger talking point and things slowly began to change.

Racism Worldwide

Lots of people arrived in Britain from the Indian sub-continent and the islands of the West Indies. Some white people found it hard to accept new races in their midst and were prejudiced against these new British citizens.

In America black people fought for more civil rights, and there were serious race riots. In South Africa there was a policy called "apartheid" aimed at keeping black and white people apart.

TV and Radio in Britain

TV shut down in the morning, afternoon and late evening. Some shows that started then are still on – Blue Peter and Top of the Pops, for example.

Pop radio stations got more popular and Radio One was launched by the BBC. Meanwhile, unlicensed "pirate" radio stations started up and were widely listened to by young people.

Everyone Out!

In the 1960s workers often went on strike, led by their unions to demand better pay and working conditions.

Nuclear Weapons and Spies

The Communist countries of eastern Europe were seen as a dangerous enemy by the Western world. Both sides gathered more and more nuclear weaponry and there were several 1960s spy scandals.

1960s TIMELINE

Here are a few of the important events of the decade. If you know someone who was alive in the 1960s, test them on their memory by reading out the news and asking them to guess which year it happened.

1960

- The movie *Ben Hur* won ten Oscars.
- John F. Kennedy became American President.
- An American spy plane called a U2 was shot down by the Russians.

1961

- President Kennedy announced plans to put the first man on the moon.
- The Berlin Wall was built, splitting Berlin in half between Communist East Germany and democratic West Germany.
- Russian Yuri Gagarin became the first human in space.

1962

- Film star Marilyn Monroe died.
- A satellite called Telstar transmitted the first pictures to television screens via space.
- Russia and America went to the brink of nuclear war over whether Russia would be allowed to base missiles in Cuba. In the end Russia did not put its missiles there.

- Nelson Mandela was jailed in South Africa. He was the black leader of the African National Congress, which was fighting against apartheid.

1963

- President Kennedy was shot dead.
- The Great Train Robbery: British thieves got away with over a million pounds, then the biggest theft ever.

1964

- There was civil war between Greeks and Turks in Cyprus.
- The new American President Johnson signed the Civil Rights Act, giving more rights to American black people.
- The Beatles visited America.
- China tested her first atomic bomb.

1965

- The Beatles got MBEs (Member of the British Empire medals).
- Capital punishment (crimes being punished by death) was ended in Britain.
- America was sending more and more troops to help South Vietnam fight North Vietnam. There were anti-war protests in America.

1966

- England won the World Cup.
- Briton Francis Chichester was the first solo round-the-world sailor.
- The first photos of Earth from space were taken.

1967

- Israelis fought Arabs in the Six-Day War over occupation of Jerusalem.
- The first heart transplant operation took place.
- The summer of 1967 was nicknamed the summer of Love because hippy art, styles of dress and music made the news.

1968

- In America both Martin Luther King and Bobby Kennedy (John Kennedy's brother) were assassinated.
- Russian tanks rolled into Czechoslovakia to re-establish Communist rule.

1969

- Neil Armstrong became the first human to walk on the moon.
- Beatle John Lennon and his new wife Yoko Ono sat in bed for a week as a peace protest.
- The population of Biafra, Africa, faced mass starvation after war with Nigeria.

Glossary

Here are some explanations of words that have appeared in this book.

Beatles

The world-famous pop group whose members were Paul McCartney, John Lennon, George Harrison and Ringo Starr.

Biba

A trend-setting London clothes shop.

Bob

A nickname for a shilling. For instance, "three bob" meant three shillings.

Carnaby Street

A London street lined with trendy fashion boutiques. It became world famous.

Chippie

A fish and chip shop – almost the only kind of take-away food shop at the time.

Dance Hall

A hall where groups played live music for people to dance to. There were no discos until the 1970s.

Dollybird

Sixties slang for a pretty girl.

Go-go Boots

Short plastic ankle boots, often white, worn by girls. Boys wore short black slip-on Beatle boots.

Hippy

A style of dressing, art and music that became popular in 1967.

Mary Quant

A famous 1960s fashion designer who made the miniskirt popular.

Op-art

A popular design style using bold colours and geometric shapes.

Psychedelic

Brightly-coloured swirling patterns popular from 1967 onwards.

Scooters

Small motorised bikes such as Vespas, very popular with 1960s teenagers.

Shilling

A unit of money in the 1960s. There were twelve pennies in a shilling.

Threads

Slang for clothes.

Twiggy

The most famous model of the 1960s. She launched her career in 1966. She was known for her boyish look.

Vietnam War

Americans sent troops to South Vietnam to try to prevent communist North Vietnam taking control of the whole area. The war escalated in 1965. Eventually America pulled out and the last American troops left in 1975.

Other titles in this series

The diary of a Young Roman Soldier

Marcus Gallo travels to Britain with his legion to help pacify the wild Celtic tribes.

The diary of a Young Tudor Lady-in-Waiting

Young Rebecca Swann joins her aunt as a lady-in-waiting at the court of Queen Elizabeth the First.

The diary of a Victorian Apprentice

Samuel Cobbett becomes an apprentice at a factory making steam locomotives.

The diary of a Young Nurse in World War II

Jean Harris is hired to train as a nurse in a London hospital just as World War II breaks out.

The diary of a Young Elizabethan Actor

William Savage is a boy actor during the last years of the reign of Queen Elizabeth the First.

The diary of a Young Soldier in World War I

It is 1914 and Billy Warren and his mates have signed up to go to France and fight in World War I.

The diary of a Young West Indian Immigrant

It is 1957 and Gloria Charles travels from Dominica in the West Indies to start a new life in Britain.